EXISTENTIAL PARADISE

Published by Spines
ISBN: 979-8-89569-279-0

EXISTENTIAL PARADISE

ZURI A. GANDY

CHAPTER 1

I can't remember why I am standing here, but the sound of the waves crashing against the rocks is soothing. The light breeze across my face and the smell of fresh seawater was very enticing; as a child, I was always drawn to water, almost like we were connected. I can remember crouching down and looking into the crystal-clear water at my reflection. I was smiling; I believe that was the first time I realized my existence in this realm. That memory of my childhood: the sky was bright blue with a few clouds dancing by, but where I was standing, the sky was dark and cold. The crescent moon was my only guide as I stood before it, glaring so intensely as if mocking me. I looked down into the water and saw the reflection of the moon. I wondered if the sun looked the same way when I was a kid; did it also reflect off the water? I couldn't remember, but I desired to escape. I wanted the freedom that water has; it can go everywhere and be everything. All this time, I stood over this body of water and didn't realize how loud the cars were; motors were loud and honking as they flew past me. I was so focused that I couldn't hear anything; the only thing I could pay attention to was the water. My mother once told me that the moon and water are spiritually connected. They both need each other; they were made for each other.

For some reason, water started pouring down my face, but it wasn't supposed to rain today, so I wiped my face, but the water wouldn't stop. I screamed into the water and yelled with a crack in my voice, "How can I become free like you?! Why do I have to be alone with nothing? With no one?" I was sobbing. Suddenly, I was falling, but I don't remember what happened. Did I trip? Was I pushed? Did I jump? It felt like I was falling for eternity into the dark abyss of the cold water below me. It was terrifying, yet I embraced my faint. I curled myself into a ball and tucked my head into my arms to protect myself, hoping that I would survive the impact. Then I was cold and couldn't see anything, my body limp, drifting down into the water. The pitch blackness stretched on forever, and it seemed never to end. I tried to look up, but couldn't feel my body for some reason. All my strength was gone. I thought to myself, "Is this the end?" Before I fell, my chest was hurting so badly, like I was being suffocated. But now everything feels light and peaceful. I lacked faith in the idea of the water protecting me from harm, but I slowly started to accept the water. As the water filled my lungs, I grasped my throat and gasped for air, bubbles forming as I struggled. I could hear a faint voice above, and it kept getting louder. It was a man's voice screaming, and he shouted, "He jumped; Jesus Christ, that boy jumped off the bridge! Somebody get help!" My inner dialogue was shocked with disbelief. "What?" I jumped, I said, puzzled. I had figured I was pushed, but apparently, I jumped, and now I am drowning. The drift between consciousness and reality was shifting, and I could no longer hold on to this vessel I call my body. I closed my eyes and lost all ability to function. I wasn't in any pain, but apparently, a lot of my bones were broken, so that's why I couldn't swim back up to the surface.

Someone kept shouting at me, "Hey, kid! When are you going to get up?" I slowly opened my eyes, and the sun instantly blinded me. I was in disbelief and looked around. I was lying on the sand, looking into the bright blue sky as seagulls flew past my head. It was beautiful. I sat up, and my mouth dropped in disbelief; the sea was sparkling and stretched on for miles, or maybe even forever. It was a rich, deep color blue that I had never seen before, and everything left me speechless. Of course, until that man ruined the moment. "So, you done sightseeing?" he said. I looked at him with discontent. "Who are you, and why are you bothering me?" I scowled at him. But then, as I looked around, I realized we were all alone. "Wait, where am I?" I asked, confused. He smiled warmly. "I am your spirit guide, and I have come to take you to the rest of your family," he explained. "What!" "Spirit guide!" "Why would I need someone or something like that?" I jumped up directly onto both feet in complete shock. "You don't remember," said my spirit guide softly. "Remember…" I felt like I was choking on the water all over again, and an overwhelming sense of grief and misery started to consume me. Suddenly, the once paradise-like place turned grim, the blue skies turned gray, and the sea violently thrashed around. The wind was so loud and deafening that it felt like I couldn't escape the chaos. I started screaming hysterically, "I'm drowning, somebody help me!" as I embraced myself, shaking uncontrollably. My spirit guide walked over and started gently holding me, patting my head and telling me that everything would be okay now, that I was safe.

The paradise slowly started to return as I became more emotionally stable, and I asked my spirit guide why everything had become so intense suddenly. "This place is your inner world; everyone's dimension looks different when you are going through something. It reflects your feelings." "Your inner world is replicating your soul," he explained. "Well, what are you?" I asked, perplexed. "Because you don't look human," I said as I put my finger on my chin, investigating this odd figure. "Wait! "My family is here?" I quickly changed the subject. "Humans are spiritual beings on a journey to fulfill a desire or a task that they need to complete. Once you are separated from the human world, you have a choice on whether to stay here or go back to the human realm to see your family," this strange figure explained. I was confused. "Why can't I do both?" I asked. "Because all your family members decided to go back and be reincarnated." "Their desires weren't accomplished because they died too soon, so your mother, father, and little sister returned to the human world once more," he elaborated. "But, mister, I don't remember much, and for some reason, I can't remember my family," I said expressionlessly. "Yes, I noticed your soul has become fractured," he said. "Your memories are trapped within because of how your death occurred." "How did I die?" I asked. "I cannot say any further because continued stress can cause more damage to your soul, which causes you to become a demon," he said, seriousness in his voice. "Well, can you at least tell me who I was in the human world?" I said with annoyance in my voice. "Your name was Noah, and you were 12 years old," he spoke. "My name is Noah!" "Wow, my parents picked a cool name!" Noah said with a huge smile. "How long have I been lying here on the beach, spirit?" Noah wondered. "Time does not exist in this realm, nor in the human realm either; it is a construct formed by the human desire to keep track of one's lifespan. It gives a sense of control over one's environment," the spirit guide explained. "Well, what do I do now since I can't go home?" Noah said with a sad expression on his face. "You heal; once you are finished, it will return and offer you the same choice." Before Noah could ask any more questions, the spirit disappeared. "Wait! "I still have more questions; come back!" As Noah cried out, crawling on the sand, one hand trying to grasp onto nothingness. "Stupid spirit, how am I supposed to heal if I don't know how I died?" Noah complained. "I have nothing; I am all alone," Noah said with heaviness in his heart. He lay back down on the warm sand, and a gentle breeze caressed his face. Noah, lying face up and staring endlessly into the sunlight and few clouds that glided by, wondered how long he had to stay in this existential paradise.

I thought about how my continued delay here has affected things; in the other realms, I would eventually be able to escape, but this world is different from where I came from. You have no choice but to face your problems. Although time doesn't exist, the act of gaining knowledge continues to expand, and eventually, I get enough to understand what I am and why I'm here. My inner dimension has yet to collapse because I have yet to give up on remembering who I was so that I may continue to experience what I lost. I pondered my purpose, considering those above and below me, but I was still unsure of where I came from or which direction I must continue toward. My spirit guide left me, and now I must continue my journey all by myself; it feels like he's been gone for a very long time, but he said, "Time doesn't exist, so maybe he never left or never existed. No one came here with me, so I figured that I died alone, or maybe when you die, you're by yourself regardless. I was once a 12-year-old boy, yet when I looked into the water at my reflection, I didn't see a 12-year-old boy." I saw a young man with no face, yet somehow, I still have expressions. It's almost like I was partially erased from existence. I don't understand why I have to suffer all alone; if this is supposed to be my soul, so bright and so warm, why is it so empty? Where are the trees or animals? It's just water and sand. There are no fish in the water. It's just clear, and it sparkles because of the sunlight. It's always shining, and darkness never appears unless my emotions become unstable. But what are emotions? What significance do they have at this moment when I no longer exist? I am in between two realms that I am restricted from because of my damaged soul. My imperfections have caused me to remain in a stagnant state of constant and utter despair, yet there's light. There are no options here. You must heal, but what is healing? I decided to get up again and look at my reflection; I was bewildered by what I saw on the water. I was no longer a young man but now an older man. Still, I could not recognize the person I was looking at. I'm unsure if that's what I look like, who I was, or my purpose; I am lost.

I walked around for a while and started playing in the sand like a child building a sandcastle. I ran to the sea's edge to scoop up some water for the sandcastle I was building, and when I bent down, I looked at my reflection in the water. I saw a young boy, and he had a face! I remembered this face; this was Noah! Noah loved the beach, and his family visited the same beach every year for his birthday. I recognized this face and chose to remain in the form of this young child to recover my memories. But this younger body was difficult to move in because I couldn't move as fast, and everything seemed so much bigger. I shuffled to the water because I had the strange urge to go deeper. It was as if I was attracted to something that was calling me. I went too far into the water and started to panic, and then I fell into the water, and I was scared. I instinctively held my breath for as long as I could, and then, as soon as I couldn't hold it anymore, I let go and expected to drown. But surprisingly, I could breathe underwater. It wasn't dark; I could see everything. It was beautiful. There was so much happening around me—giant fish that I thought weren't there, but I was always been too scared to go in the water. Streaks of sunlight pierced the water, glistening off fish scales and the blue-colored coral. I decided to venture even more into the sea and discovered a box. It was small, so I was able to pick it up. I was curious about what was inside, so I immediately opened it. I've been so bored and alone for so long. Finally, I found something exciting. In that box were my memories; apparently, I had buried them deep in the sea because I was too afraid to relive what I went through in my experience in the human realm. I feared the water, so it was a perfect hiding spot. The only part of me that had enough courage to go down and retrieve my memories was the kid version of Noah. I instantly remembered what had happened to me and my family. In many religious texts, ending your own life is considered a sin, and now I understand why: because it damages your soul and can make it difficult to move on to your next journey.

As humans, we are all interconnected but placed on different expeditions. Everyone will have obstacles in their lives; it's a part of the quest, no matter the experience one goes through. Ending it abruptly can cause complications for Noah… or me… or us… it ended too soon. I swam back to the shore because I knew it was waiting for me. "So, you have healed?" the figure spoke; it was strange because it was once unfamiliar and strange, but now it looked normal. It was as if it had changed, or did I change? "Yes, I think so," I said softly. "Why do I feel so different now?" I asked, and it said, "It's because you have your memories back." "You don't have a real name, but you have gone by many names." It was right; when my memories were restored, I realized Noah wasn't my name, and I had many faces. I could not recognize those other faces in the reflection of the water because Noah never had a chance to mature. "Have you made your decision?" the figure asked. It wanted to know if I wanted to be reincarnated or stay here. Usually, this decision would not be difficult because when a human vessel dies, it was pre-planned ahead of time, but ending one's own life isn't a part of the plan. Because my soul was damaged, I brought human emotions into the space between the spirit and the living world. I am no longer linked with the human world, but I still have the memories of Noah's pain. He suffered greatly, and I feel like it is unfair that he did not get to complete his life, and I was unable to finish my true desire. I desired to understand how to overcome loneliness. I wanted to know what it felt like; that burning sensation of isolation intrigued me, so I asked to become someone who suffers and wishes to connect with someone. Noah was crying out for help and running to the bridge. He figured someone would come and save him, but no one noticed until he jumped. Everyone just walked past and was more worried about themselves. Noah lost his entire family in an accident, was placed in foster care at the age of 10, and spiraled into a deep depression. "Where did I go wrong on my mission?" I asked the figure. "Human emotions are complex and are that way for survival," it spoke. "Have you made your decision?" it asked once again. If I were to be reincarnated once again, I would be given the same task to complete, and if I were to fail again, I risk transforming into a demonic entity.

They say those who let their human desires and emotions consume them risk expulsion into the realm of purgatory to be forcibly cleansed. It is not something we fear, but it wipes away everything we learn, and basically, we have to start all over again from scratch. We are placed on this earth with goals to pursue, guiding us toward becoming beings who truly understand humanity and spirituality. We have a different time coexisting as one, separated by the sins created by demons. Keeping humans from reaching their full potential, some humans try to practice the art of connecting with the spiritual realms. Unfortunately, most do it incorrectly, and many unknowingly worship the demon realm. Sins are pushed to the limit in these communities, where a leader controlled by demons leads individuals into disarray. "I don't want to be reincarnated; I want to stay here and become a spirit guide," I said with burning passion. Once blank and shapeless, my form took on the shape of Noah at the same age when he died. I was amazed as I looked down at my hands. "I turned back into a human?" I shouted. "What? I can express myself, and my emotions are back, but why?" I said, perplexed. The only difference was the wings on my back. They were a rich blue and sparkled like the water surrounding us. "This will be your form now," said the figure. "But why? I didn't want to be reincarnated," I said with annoyance. "You were able to gain some enlightenment in becoming a complete being, but you are still lacking in some areas, so your transformation is incomplete." "Also, you are at a higher risk of being sent to the realm of purgatory because you are more susceptible to sin." "You may choose who you want to help on their journey, and because of your stronger connections to humans, your blessing will be more powerful." "Therefore, "You need to use your powers with greater responsibility," the figure said with authority in his voice. My original spirit guide decided to find a soul, so the figure I am speaking to now is something different. This figure is considered a perfect being in the human realm. He goes by many names: the universe, God, our Lord, and sometimes our savior. To us, he is everything and nothing; we are it, and it is us; we are nothing but mere fractions of this greater being. Although this being is perfect, it cannot enter the human realm, so it must stay here, and it sends us to help retrieve information and gain knowledge against the war of demons and spirits.

CHAPTER 3

$\mathcal{I}$ no longer wanted to be reincarnated, and because of my decision, I have become an incomplete holy being who has been given a task to help others reach their full potential. Very few beings exist in this form, and they don't last long, as they fall, succumb to sin, and lose all connection to the spirit realm. Having the ability to experience human pleasure and suffer no consequences leads one to become corrupted, and this causes chaos in the human realm. Many children are born from this imperfect being and tend to be more spiritually gifted than regular humans, which is considered a sin. The act of procreation is a sacred experience, and an imperfect being can destroy a human's connection to other humans. I find those types of people interesting, and I decided to link myself to a gifted being. "I'm leaving now," I said to it. "Oh! Already you have picked someone?" it asked. "Yes, a newborn is going to be born in a few minutes, and I want to guide that spirited hybrid," I said with deep focus. "A corrupted offspring, fascinating; usually, spirits don't guide them," it proclaimed. It was telling the truth. We see no need to protect those beings because they have spiritual powers and are deemed unworthy of protection. Solely based on how they were conceived, they are left to fend for themselves. Because they lack protection, many become tortured and turn to isolation, slowly transforming into wicked beings. This curse can last for generations, all due to the actions of one imperfect being who couldn't control their desires. With my newfound human emotions, I can empathize with their existence and wish to help. I will be the first spirit guide to assist a being in misfortune, even though I am an incomplete spirit myself. I descended into the human realm and awaited my first human. I decided to wait in the corner of the hospital ward and listen to their cries. I forgot how loud and busy the human world was; it was almost overwhelming. I covered my ears with my hands to block out some of the noise, and a sense of fear crept up my spine. "What kind of feeling is this?" I whispered to myself. Then, everything was silent. It was as if the room was spinning around me, and the only noise I could hear was a baby crying. My eyes suddenly filled with tears of happiness and distress. I flew around in joy that my being was born; I could feel her heartbeat and every breath she took. The pain and fear I felt was her birth, but now she is free, and I get to guide her for the rest of her life. Because spirits need time to adjust to their human forms, they can still communicate with other spirits once the connection is established.

However, their memories remain repressed until they leave the human realm.

I flew over to my being; she was lying in a basket coddled in thick fluffy blankets, and asked what her name was, "Hello, I am your spirit guide; my name is Noah," I said with a silly grin. I got a good look at her and noticed she had dark black curly hair, tanned skin, and deep gray eyes that seemed as dazzling as the night sky. "Noah?" she said; spirits have names now? She said with shock in her inner dialogue. "I was given the name Talia." She spoke. "That's a pretty name!" I said with excitement. Talia looked confused at our spirit guide because he looked odd. This spirit was unusual, addressing himself with the title of Noah; his form is in the shape of a human vessel. Long silver braided hair into one French braid, bright blue eyes were like looking into the ocean, slightly golden-skinned, and had a glorious smile that seemed to light up the room. He couldn't be any older than 10 or 11, yet he stood before me with wings shimmering like the blue sky. What kind of mystic being is this? "What are you? And why do you look like a human?" asked Talia. "I am a spirit guide, but I am also a spirit who has acquired human emotions; we are called semi-imperfect beings," Noah explained. Talia had every right to be curious because imperfect beings are rare and don't live long. Also, Talia is a corrupted offspring from a few generations ago. One of her ancestors was an imperfect being. Gaining a spirit guide has not occurred in this family for many years. "What sin did you commit to become this imperfect being"? asked Talia in a tone that felt like she was damning to the realm of purgatory. Rare doesn't mean unknown; rare means bad in this context. "I took my own life, which brought human emotions into the dimension between the living and the spirit realm. I chose to become a spirit guide instead of being reincarnated." I said it in a soft and sorrowful tone. My Talia was visually irritated by my existence, as though I was scum, a sinful abomination that dear to approach her and state the words "spirit guide" in a serious tone. But I couldn't blame her disgust towards me; I chose to continue my life in sin instead of being reincarnated. I let human emotions control my judgment and developed an ego that believed he deserved to continue living.

In truth, I was afraid and weak as an imperfect being. I am now lower than any human or spirit, and I am closer to being a demon ready to succumb to sin. The same feeling of loneliness that only a human can feel, I can now feel, and this is a sin. Sin is distinct in the human world: good vs. evil, the yin and yang, the positive and the negative. These opposites have their sides and work together to create balance. All human emotions are balanced, while spirits lack emotions. A spirit with emotions is a hidden, chaotic being with no balanced emotions, depending on how the death of a spirit is left with the emotions of that incomplete human. Soon, my mind will take over, darkness will consume my very being, and I will become a demon. Before, becoming a demon wasn't scary, but now, as an imperfect being, I am petrified of losing who I am. But who am I? We spirits don't have names, but I call myself "Noah." The inconsistency in my thinking will forever be a sinful reminder of my decisions. There is no beating in my chest, yet it feels tight and difficult to breathe. Are these my emotions or Noah's? I started looking down at my hands, frozen in place, pondering. Talia was looking at me with a blank expression. "Are you going to cry? Isn't that my job?" she said with a smirk. My head quickly rose, and my eyes widened with acceptance and glee. "Of course not!" Noah said with a smile and sniffled, rubbing his eyes into his arm. "My memories will soon fade, so I do not need to hold a grudge against your decisions. I do wonder how long you will last in this realm until you succumb to sin," she pondered. "I am not sure, and I fear my inevitable future, but I wish to protect you until I can ensure you that your life will be safe in my hands," Noah said proudly. As Talia traveled home with her parents, Noah followed behind with so many mixed emotions; the thought of the future terrified him, but there was this burning desire to continue; he wanted to see the next chapter in his life as Talia's spirit guide.

CHAPTER 4

Talia and her parents arrived home: a two-story brick house surrounded by trees. The new family slowly walks into the falling leaves, falls off the trees, and starts circling them. The sun's light dances through the crowns of the trees. That moment seemed to last forever, but in the blink of an eye, Talia was ten and going to school. She was a bright child with a unique talent for seeing other spirits; when she realized no one else could see them, she quickly hid her skill and decided to depict her sights through art. She would paint these lovely pictures of me and, along with other spirits, humans refer to them as ghosts. But Talia also saw demons as well, and she referred to them as monsters. She drew only one picture of a demonic spirit, and it horrified her parents. Talia's father was disturbed, but her mother was visually horrified. Their family's curse is known as the devil's artist, where a child is born and is gifted the ability to produce the most wonderful and detailed painting, but there is a cost: the child goes mad and usually dies of a strange and unknown disease. The family calls it a painter's stroke, but Talia is too young, so her parents decide to tell her when she gets older. As a spirit guide, I am not supposed to interact with my being unless I am needed, but it isn't easy when she can see you. "Hello, spooky ghost!" said Talia with a huge grin, missing several teeth. I ignored her as usual and kept my distance, but it was nice to receive her greeting; it made me not feel alone. "Why do you never talk? Talia pouted. "Why can't I see others like you?" Talia's curiosity was expanding. Talia noticed that I did not look like the other spirits around her; I was indeed unique. At school, Talia was a normal little girl with friends and even a crush on a boy named Lucian. She excelled in her classes and loved getting rough with the boys during physical training. Her favorite class was art class, and because she was so talented, she was moved up to the advanced art classes with the older children. Everyone was amazed by her gift of drawing. Talia's teacher recommended that she enter into an art contest that she was guaranteed to win. She was hesitant, so I gave her some motivational words: "You're a wonderful painter; believe in yourself." I spoke softly. Talia's face lit up with astonishment. "I'll do it!" Said Talia with power in her voice. Later that same day, Talia told her parents about the art contest; both were visually concerned but tried to hide it as best they could. Talia ran upstairs to start painting. "I am going to draw you again, but this time, even better!" she spoke directly to me, and her expression was between intense passion and apprehension. "Why did you talk to me in class?" Talia asked while facing me, picking the right colors to draw. I answered, "Because it is my job as your spirit guide." I spoke. Talia dropped everything in awe as this was the first time I had spoken to her since she was an infant. "My name is Noah, and I have been watching over you since birth." I started, and before she could ask me any more questions, I left and rested on the roof. Talia wasn't upset by my disappearance; she picked up her paintbrush and started painting with even more enthusiasm than usual. I began to understand that deep down, Talia also felt alone, locked in a world of her own, unable to indeed be herself in the fear of rejection. Talia could feel the other kids envying her artwork and sense the fear in her parents when she talked about her artwork. We are the same; Talia and I were looked at by others with disgust and forced into solitude. We cannot fully be ourselves, for if we were to sin, the consequences would follow. I like the idea of morning and night here in the earthly realm; it gives you time to enjoy the day and rest at night. Being that I am an imperfect being, I stay up all night thinking about my sins, wondering when the gates of Hell will open before me. Will I plead for forgiveness or accept my fate? Will I let sin control my desires, or will I become a cleansed spirit once again? My ego, will, and drive to live are strong, which is my sin. I am nothing but a mere spirit guide, yet I see value in my life; I question myself, but It didn't care, or maybe he couldn't care. Why am I asking things like I am human? Questioning everything around me, I am nothing, not a human or a spirit. I call myself Noah, but that is not my name; I am nameless, so why do I hold on to this name so dearly? What is the significance of this name? I wonder, with this name that I have stolen, which sin might taint it with pride—envy or greed? Only time will tell what act I commit against this name in vain. Today was Talia's art competition; usually, I have an unfortunate nihilistic tone, but I was genuinely excited. Talia looked nervous, so I decided to stand by her, which boosted her confidence; her friends, art teacher, and parents also supported her. The painting was breathtaking; I noticed she had named the art piece. Looking closer, I realized it wasn't called Noah but was given the name "Atman." Why did she name a painting of me and not put the name I go by? It was confusing, but humans are strange creatures. The judges made their way over to Talia's painting and looked mesmerized by the artwork. One judge asked, "What was your inspiration?" Another interrupted and asked, "Why did you name it 'Atman'? Is there a reason or a purpose?" Both judges stood waiting for their questions to be answered. Talia was overwhelmed but did her best to answer their questions. "Well, the image came to me in a dream; I consider this boy my spirit guide." I picked Atman because it means soul or 'self.' We are two different beings coexisting together, and I wanted to represent that in my artwork," she said. I shouted, "Names have meaning!" I caught Talia off guard, but she did her best not to react to my outburst. The judges, puzzled at her odd demeanor, gave their scores and left. I apologized, but Talia was more amused than angry about my behavior.

She chose that name because she didn't believe "Noah" fit my personality. She said I was a special, one-of-a-kind guardian sent to protect her and was grateful for my existence. I could not face her after such kind words. I flew away, hid under some shaded trees, and cried. For so long, I've been alone, wishing for this misery to end, waiting for my demise. This is why humans are so unique: they find meaning in nothingness and cherish it. Even with all these emotions, humans can excel, maybe because of these feelings. I once felt so ashamed of these human emotions that I hid them as much as possible. I am questioning who is guiding me or my darling human, Talia. She claims we are interconnected; whether that will become my ultimate sin, damning me to hell, I am not sure, but regardless, I will be by my human's side.

CHAPTER 5

The longer I stay in the human realm, the more I appreciate its charming qualities. I find human life captivating in every menial task they do with such focus and methodical precision. The simple task of making one's meal requires many parts; humans do not simply see an edible object and eat it. They must always perform a ritual before consumption. First, they gather the items, clean them, and prepare the food using various methods. Finally, they set the items on fire. After all that, their meal is finally complete, and within a few minutes, everything is gone. All that manual labor for sustenance, but the humans look so fulfilled and satiated by preparing their meals multiple times daily. I enjoy watching my human cook; apparently, art skills are not limited to one subject, and one can use one's gift in many ways. Talia bakes and likes to decorate her pastries; although I cannot eat them, her craft smells lovely. I decided to see what

Talia was making; the few times, I wished to be a complete holy being. "Smells exquisite," I said, flying as if the aroma lifted me off the ground. "Why, thank you, Noah," Talia said with a smile. My human is exceptional; protecting such a rare being is truly an honor. "I wish you could have some; sadly, you can't eat human food," she said while pulling freshly baked goods out of the oven. Moments later, Talia's parents walked in, and by the look on their faces, it was something serious. Talia's mother asked her to meet them in the living room when she was finished. With mild hesitation, Talia agreed to their request to speak.

The family gathered in the living room, and both of Talia's parents sat across from her and, with an intense gaze, started whispering to their daughter. Her father said, "Talia, you are almost 15; time is flying by. I remember when you were just an infant curled in my arms." It looked like her father was about to cry, but he collected himself quickly. Talia's mother shifted the conversation: "Talia, we wanted to discuss the family curse inherited every few generations. We probably should have told you years ago, but we were too scared to cause you any pain. Usually, anyone on my side of the family who is blessed with artistic skills doesn't live long. You are the oldest who has lived this long. I don't know how much time you have left, and I am terrified to lose you." She said, trembling with tears flowing uncontrollably. Talia's mother and father embraced each other, unable to look Talia in the face in fear of her expression. "I'll be okay," said Talia, reassuring to her parents. Talia's parents look up at her, baffled by her claim. They wondered if she was trying to protect their feelings. Then Talia said, "My spirit guide has been protecting me! So, you don't need to worry," she said with a huge smile. Talia showed her parents her painting from the art contest that she won and said, "This is what he looks like; isn't he wonderful." But her parents had every reason to be concerned for their daughter's well-being because it is true Talia shouldn't be alive; the demons should have devoured her soul a long time ago. But my presence keeps them away, and I am more powerful than the average spirit. Although I am seen as a threat, it puts a target on my back. As soon as sin taints my soul, the demons will consume my essence and then take my human's life force. Talia's parents knew she had a gift and had to believe what she was saying because she was still alive; her parents were mystified. They couldn't see me, but they both decided to get done and bow, thanking me for protecting their daughter. I was humbled by their kindness towards me and tried my best to hold back tears of happiness. After that day, Talia's parents prayed to me every night; they called me by the name given to me by Talia.

"I pray my daughter continues to be protected by the ultimate being, Atman; please watch over her and keep her safe. Protect her from harm and guide her with your loving care. Amen."

CHAPTER 6

As long as I can remember, I have never truly felt alone. Some of my earliest memories were of me lying awake in my crib and seeing dancing, multi-colored shadows, some with faces and others without. I would reach out to these figures, and many would play with me while others would try to talk to me. As I grew older, those shadows became easier to see, and that's when I noticed Noah. He looked different from the spirits that surrounded me; he was beautiful. Noah never left my side. It didn't matter what I was doing. He was nearby, watching my every move. For some reason, he never scared me; I always felt safe around him, as if he was protecting me from someone or something. I had a passion for drawing, and as soon as I could hold a crayon, Noah was the first person I wanted to draw. I kept drawing so that one day, I could fully capture his pure essence and grace; while his expression never changed, I sensed a deep, aching sadness. I had hoped that one day, I could put a smile on his face. I tried my best to get Noah's attention as the years passed. I wanted to know everything about him and why he always followed me around. He never responded, but it was evident that I could see him; he never spoke, just stayed close by my side. But I guess I couldn't complain because I was never alone, and neither was he. Noah always looked lonely. I realized I was different from everyone else at age 5 when I noticed other people didn't see spirits, and I would scare my parents and other children with my drawings. That first school year was lonely because everyone thought I was weird, but it was okay because Noah was close by, so I would talk to him, although he wouldn't respond. Luckily, kids have short attention spans, and by the following year, I could restart the school year strong. I decided never to speak about spirits, especially the dark ones, ever again. One day, Noah talked to me, and I was ecstatic because it was the first time I heard his voice; it was so majestic. He sounded like a little choir boy but spoke with maturity and wisdom. It took a while, but we were able to build a bond, and now I see Noah express different emotions all the time; he seems a lot happier. But I still don't know anything about him or his past: What is he, and why does he look human? I have seen many spirit guides around others, but they do not look like Noah. Why is Noah so special? And why was he gifted to me? I sometimes wonder if Noah could ever become fully human, but I know that's a silly thought; Noah is obviously one of God's angels. But if Noah is genuinely one of God's seraphs, why would he be here with me? Why would he always look so crestfallen, as if God had forsaken him? I know I need Noah because he protects me, but I have this burning desire to understand his real purpose, even if I risk losing my life. Although Noah has a job protecting me, he seems so sad, and I don't want to be the reason for his misery. Am I causing his despair, or is it God, or is he battling inner demons far too complex for the human mind to comprehend? It feels strange to have such a deep connection with someone but know so little about them, yet I am afraid to ask him questions. Where is this fear arising from? A pit of anxiety started to form in my stomach, a feeling of uncertainty and selfish desire. I am nothing but a pitiful human being who lacks God's blessing. I was destined to be consumed by demons, yet I questioned my protector. I am an unholy beast who is undeserving of redemption. But I must know because I have a thirst for knowledge regarding the spirit that watches over me, the spirit who calls himself "Noah."

That night, the eve of my seventeenth year, I asked my holy guardian about his past. What I learned would forever change my perspective on those whom ordinary humans cannot see. I would learn about another sacred realm different from my own, where our free will is tested, but the wrong choice could lead to an eternity of suffering. I slightly hesitated when I spoke, but I mustered up the strength to call Noah, who was always nearby; he quickly appeared and answered, "You called?" "My lady Talia." "I am sorry for bothering you this late evening, but I have a request." "I wanted to learn more… about you and where you came from." "We've known each other for so long, yet... you still feel like a stranger." "I know, I know I have no right to ask... you these questions, but you are special to me, and I want to hear your story!" I shouted. I quickly covered my mouth, realizing I had spoken too loudly, and prayed I didn't wake up my parents. Noah always had such a calm demeanor, so it wasn't easy to guess his thoughts. I was standing, looking toward Noah; he had nestled himself into my window alcove, back pressed against the cool glass, legs curled up close to his chest. One arm rested casually on the windowsill, fingers idly tracing patterns on the cold surface. "My dear Talia, would you think of a failed being like me?" It's a simple request, yet I feel some shame and doubt. Could a simple human understand the complexities of another world? But my Talia is different. She is also a cursed being, just like I am. It must be a cold night because I can see Talia shivering due to the window opening; she went over to her bed, grabbed a blanket, sat on her bed, and looked defeated. I felt terrible for not wanting to move, but being close to the window gave me a sense of freedom. Although I can go through objects now, this window symbolizes escapism. The fear of complete isolation again worries me deeply; I do not have a comforting item like a soft, warm piece of cloth to caress against my cheek or a stuffed animal to cuddle while I sleep. I can't touch anything or anyone. I do not sleep, eat, or dream; my only purpose is to be a protector. But I can feel my ego taking over and demonic thoughts trying to assume control. They try to convince me that if I let them combine with my imperfect form, I can become a human, granting me all earthly desires. I knew this day would come when I could no longer bear a real connection; humans have so many needs fulfilled by their inner community.

To have no one is its form of purgatory. It is a blessing and a curse to experience being a human; maybe becoming an ultimate being will never be possible. Perhaps this is a twisted charade veiled as the primary goal. These thoughts can only be expressed through human emotions and a pure soul. The irony lies in desiring the will of God while defying His way of ruling. I speak as if God is bad or good; only in the human realm is God labeled as a supreme being who is all-knowing and altruistic. In contrast, demons are spirits who have forsaken their Lord and Savior and are condemned to hell, where they must burn and suffer for eternity. But that doesn't make any sense. Why does God get to choose others' fate if He is neither good nor bad? Why do humans see God this way? After sitting in silence for a while, I finally decided to speak. "My name isn't Noah; all spirits are nameless." But I have grown rather fond of this name and have chosen to go by this name." "I have lived many lives, more than any human can ever comprehend." "Every human was designed by the deity you humans call 'God'; God gave humans free will to act and do as they please." One of God's most fabulous creations, He found these creatures interesting. He wanted to obtain knowledge from these beings. He created and decided to send pieces of Himself down to the earthly realm. "You know the Holy Ghost, the soul, and the spirit? Every human has a soul, and a spirit connects with them to gain information for God. Basically, spirits are God." "Spirits are separate from God but are still one and the same." "Once we gain human emotions, we become unstable." That is why our memories are erased after completing our missions. But humans can be unpredictable; that is why God is fascinated by these creatures. "That is how immoral beings like me get created: a spirit who has maintained a human's emotions, an imperfect being." "My human vessel committed a sinful act, and now I must suffer the consequences of their actions." "That boy's name was Noah, and he lost his family in a tragic accident." The silence in the room was loud, and I didn't know whether to continue or stop; I wanted to look at Talia's face to respond based on her expression, but I could not bear to face her. "What sin did your vessel commit?" Talia asked with deep sorrow. I think about Noah's death frequently and how chilling his death was, and I am basically a walking corpse parading around in his body, pretending to be human. The loneliness will never compare, but I have an unnerving sense that my ego wants me to compare, wondering who suffered more, Noah or me. I am such a dreadful being created to aid and educate but allow impure thoughts to overtake my mind. I have no room to judge Noah because I felt every emotion: fear, grief, and despair. I felt the blood running down his throat from rupturing his vocal cords, screaming for his mother in agony, suffocating from overwhelming torture. So many nights, Noah's limp body, which lacked attention and care, barely got out of bed, unable to function properly, having morbid thoughts and questioning his existence. He blamed God for taking away his family, and he wanted them back; he was only a child. That child had the idea to take his own life to be with his family again. If anything, that act should be seen as heroic, not sinful; yet I am here imprisoned in this state of damnation. Although I have obtained knowledge beyond my years, I continue to maintain this infantile form. The irony of having so much wisdom that could fill many libraries but forever being trapped in childlike body with fragile emotions that can only be soothed with comfort. I wonder if all humans feel like this. Confined within one's inferiority complex of never feeling complete, never fully omniscient, and yearning for a state where one is in a state of enlightenment would ease so much suffering; yet humans struggle to reach that pinnacle. Human life looks so modest and harmonious, but immense pain and turmoil are hidden under that simple charm. Primitive tasks, when viewed through the lens of a spirit, may seem simplistic by nature. Yet, for humans, everything is essential for survival, including one's emotional state. While humans are supported by their community when damaged emotionally or physically, Noah wasn't; what a lamentable fate.

"Noah took his life; he wanted to be with his family that he so dearly missed," I answered somberly. Talia burst into tears, covering her mouth and trying to silence herself so as not to wake her parents. "That's so heartbreaking; that poor boy was all alone. How can God be so cruel, someone who is so powerful yet lacks understanding and grace? This can't be the Lord you serve to make anyone bear the weight of someone's death. Why... must you... suffer?" she said, whimpering. "Because the boy sinned, someone must suffer a consequence for his actions," I answered. A part of me agrees with Talia, the thought of God being so cruel, but how can He be wrong? He knows all and does not have an ego or human emotions to affect His judgment; right and wrong do not exist, but taking one's life is a sin, quite contradictory, if I may say. Talia cried the rest of the night until she eventually fell asleep for the first time; I could also fall asleep. A strange feeling of exhaustion overtook me, and my eyelids became heavy. I sucked in the air many times, a response I could not control; I decided to lie next to my Talia. Being next to her felt so blissful, and I felt connected to someone for once. Is this what it feels like to feel secure? Is this how Noah wanted to feel before he took his life? A sense of calm amidst the calamity.

CHAPTER 7

"*D*reams are expressions of reality, not just products of our imagination." As a being split between worlds, this saying resonated with me as I tried to decipher my first dream. That night, I slept against my loving Talia and fell into a trance in which I pictured lovely memories of my mother. I don't remember her name, but I'll never forget her face. She had a beautiful smile that lit up a room and the voice of an angel. We were walking on the beach together, holding each other's hands. The ocean sparkled as the sun was setting, and the reflection of the multicolored sky would permanently be imprinted in my mind. There were so many colors: red, purple, orange, and pink. I let go of my mother's hand and ran toward the water with the biggest grin. I stopped as the water and sea foam came up to my knees. My mother wasn't far behind me, smiling warmly and letting me have fun in the water. I looked down at the water and noticed my reflection. The reflection had no face; it bewildered me, so I looked back at my mother for reassurance, but she wasn't there; she was gone. Suddenly, the once calm and gentle water swallowed me whole, and I was thrust into the sea, drifting further from the shore, all alone with the sun setting. The darkness took over my world, and I was again all alone, drowning in despair. Sinking into the abyss, I remember yelling, "Mommy, help me!" That's when I woke up from my dream, tears streaming down my face, and I gasped for air, marveling at the dream's verisimilitude. Feeling disheveled and overwhelmed with confusion, I started hyperventilating, grabbing my chest, trying to calm myself down. I didn't understand the tightness in my chest or the dream. What is my body trying to convey to me by forcing me to relive old memories in a twisted fashion? Looking over, Talia was still sound asleep; luckily, I did not wake her with my miserable gasping and quiet sobs. I decided to lie on the roof and wait for sunrise; I felt I had slept enough for now.

"He brought them out of darkness, the utter darkness, and broke away their chains. Let them give thanks to the Lord for his unfailing love and wonderful deeds for mankind, for he breaks down gates of bronze and cuts through bars of iron. Some became fools through their rebellious ways and suffered affliction because of their iniquities." (Psalm 107:14-17, NIV)...

Talia started studying the Bible. A person once thought to be forsaken by God saw no reason to adhere to the Lord's command. But after learning about my past, Talia's thirst for knowledge overwhelmed her so much that she started attending church every Sunday and sat in the front row. It was as if she were under a spell when watching the priest speak; his stories of mystery and mysticism enamored Talia. I was also curious to learn how humans interpret life and the God overseeing its creation; I wonder if they could handle learning about undesirables like me. My Talia wept with pity. Would others show emotion for me? Or is Talia's hubris so overwhelming that it defies worldly comprehension? Although I have many of Noah's memories, I do not have any of him attending service; I wonder if he was affiliated with a religious group that could have prevented his untimely demise, for he would have had a community to care for his well-being.

My Talia started hosting Bible studies at her house. After attending church a few times, she became close with several young ladies named Esther, who is 16 years old and attends the same school as Talia. Still, they weren't close due to having very little in common. Despite being so young, she enjoys socializing and is a very active church member. Esther is a kind, outgoing spirit with a freckled face and a warm smile. Elizabeth is 17 years old and attends an all-girls' Christian private school. She works part-time at her family's glassmaking business. In her free time, she enjoys playing chess and writing poetry. Though she can sometimes be shy, often trying to hide behind her long, curly brown hair, her unique appearance always draws attention. The demanding work of glassmaking has shaped her body, giving her a tall, slender frame with well-defined, toned muscles. Though her beauty is undeniable, it pales in comparison to my dear Talia, and her presence unnerves lesser men. Lastly, Seraphina, an 18-year-old raised in a strict household, is homeschooled and has limited social interactions to protect herself from outside influences. Despite her parents' initial reservations due to Elizabeth and Esther being present, she was allowed to join us. I genuinely enjoy Seraphina's company; her maturity and wisdom enrich our group, and our friendship has grown stronger through our time together. She has a passion for singing and leads the church choir, where her voice is often described as "angelic." With her long light brown hair always braided down her back, glasses covering her bright greenish-blue eyes, and tanned skin, she truly embodies the grace of her singing. All three of these young women welcomed Talia warmly and were intrigued by her conversion to Christianity. It was a refreshing change to see a new face in the church, as most attendees had been coming since childhood. The young ladies were curious about Talia and what led her to join the church. Although Talia's parents aren't religious, they fully support their daughter's choices. Talia's mother served tea and snacks as the young women discussed the day's service and shared laughs about their interactions with the young men. "Did you ladies see Oliver today? He cut his hair. I think I liked it better longer," said Esther. "I would have to agree; I preferred Oliver's hair longer as well," said Elizabeth. Seraphina was reading her Bible, not paying the other two ladies any attention. "Hello! Seraphina? Are you listening?" said Esther as she gently lowered Seraphina's Bible with one finger, staring directly into her face. "No, I am not. I am currently partaking in the study of my Lord; obviously, you two are shortsighted and lack grace," said Seraphina sternly. Esther and Elizabeth rolled their eyes and sighed. Esther looked at Talia and began to speak. Talia was also peacefully reading her Bible but overheard the conversation. "What do you think about Oliver, Talia?" Esther asked. Talia didn't want to answer the question because she found Oliver very handsome and charming; she got flustered whenever Oliver's name was mentioned in conversation. "Oh, I… didn't no...tic...e," said Talia shyly. Esther and Elizabeth looked at each other and smiled fiendishly. They then looked toward Talia's direction and said simultaneously, "You like Oliver, don't you, Talia?" Talia's face quickly flushed reddish-pink, and she buried her face in her Bible and started reading a page out loud, trying to ignore the question. Both young ladies snickered, and Seraphina signed, "Can we finish now?" Everyone collected themselves and finished their study session.

It was nice to see the young ladies getting along; Talia had never had too many close friends. A classmate would come over now and again, or sometimes she would be invited to a gathering to play games and indulge in copious amounts of food. Talia always enjoyed being around other children, but she was an only child due to her curse. Her parents couldn't imagine bringing another child into this world to possibly suffer the same fate. Talia, adorned and lavished by her parents, still felt alone for many years. To see her laugh and smile with glee is a genuinely heartwarming sight. I envied her; Talia and I were one and the same, lonesome, yearning for a deep connection for a long time. They say loneliness is like starvation: you don't realize how hungry you are until you begin to eat. Talia's and my friendship helped feed my empty stomach, and now I have become gluttonous. Selfishness consumes me, and I wish for nothing but to be on Talia's side; it's not enough to be in second or third place. She must choose me and only me because I crave, or rather I lust for, the emotional intimacy that only my Talia can give me, for she is superior, indeed a unique specimen that no one can compare to. This burning desire shakes me to my core. With this amount of seeded resentment toward Talia's new friends, will this cause friction in our relationship? How could I forgive myself for thinking I had the privilege to impede on Talia's social life as her spirit guide? I should be helping her, not causing more harm. I am slowly sinking in and out of the dimness; various emotions arise, none of which are positive, some of which I cannot describe. Soon, I will be consumed by wretchedness because my existence is a sin, and I have no true belonging. But if I fall to temptation, I will not be the only one to suffer; my dearest Talia will perish as well.

CHAPTER 8

$\mathcal{M}$emories are essential to humans; they help them connect to others and the environment around them, expand their knowledge, and enhance their capabilities. Skills are gained over time to ease the chore of everyday life. These memories can be valued at the same currency as gold. The human body is often compared to a machine with malfunctioning parts that must be repaired. However, the human body is weak; it can easily succumb to illness, or the mind can become sick with internal or external diseases. Compared to other species, humans seem undesirable, like cursed mammals forever stuck in cycles of rebirth and death, loneliness and disrepair. My father would say, "Earth is the real heaven; don't let anyone take you away from your paradise." That quote never made any sense; he was a professor, and I was used to him throwing out random sayings; he sure was a character. I wonder if he remembered that I wanted him to buy me a bike for my birthday; he was always so busy that he forgot the dates. An intelligent man but a terrible father, my sister would probably agree.

"Brother! Wake up! It's time for school!" yelled Noor. Noah started tossing and turning in bed. "I'm… coming," he said with his arms in the air as he stretched and yawned. The family gathered at the table to eat breakfast; Noah's mother made oatmeal and toast and laid out various fruits for everyone to pick from and enjoy. Noah sat beside his sister and grabbed an apple and his oatmeal. "Do you want a glass of milk to go with your meal, Noah?" his mother kindly asked. "No, I hate milk; you know that, Mom," said Noah, who was visibly annoyed by his mother's offer as he started shoveling oatmeal into his mouth. "I'll have milk, Mommy!" Noor yelled with a smile.

"Be kind to your mother, Noah. You need to increase your dairy intake so you can grow into a strong man," said Noah's father as he came down the steps into the kitchen.

"Good morning, dear. It's okay, silly me. I forgot that Noah doesn't like milk," said Mother.

"I want milk, Mom!" said Noor.

"No need to yell," said Father.

Mother poured a glass of milk and handed it to Noor. "Here, love," said Mother.

"It sure is a lovely day; the sky couldn't look any bluer, and those clouds are fluffy like marshmallows," said Father.

"You say that every day, Dad; even if it were raining, you'd probably say the same thing," Noah said.

"You're probably right, son, because every—

"'Day is a blessing, I know, Dad. Sheesh,'" said Noah.

Father smiled as if he couldn't be prouder. "That's right, son. I'm glad. For a while, I thought everything I was saying was going in one ear and out the other."

"You say a blessing as if you believe someone can answer your request," said Noah.

"Hmmm, interesting. As a man of God, I must disagree, but I like the way you think," said Father.

"You let us think so freely but believe in God?" said Noah.

"I want my children to be free thinkers. What's wrong with that?" shrugged the father.

"Your father is a professor, dear; I would hope he encourages free thought," said Mother.

"I thought he would be encouraging logic, not magic," said Noah.

"A wise man once said, 'The existence of God is self-evident in itself, but not to us. Therefore, it must be demonstrated by things that are more known to us, though less known in their nature—namely, the effects,'" said Father.

"Sheesh... I'm finished with breakfast. I'm off to school," said Noah.

"Brother, are we going to play today?" said Noor.

"I'm too old to play with dolls," said Noah while walking out the door.

"...Bye no—"

Noah had slammed the door before Noor could say goodbye.

"Time is an illusion, a concept created by humans; the

distinction between past, present, and future is a persistent deception." Everything felt foreign, and I hadn't recognized the differences until my dreams offered me a glimpse into the past. "The day my mother, father, and sister perished could just as well be considered the future." "The universe is infinite, yet humans remain unaware of its magnificence." "I am cursed to understand the incomprehensible, not entirely able to conceptualize." I have an eerie feeling of being trapped in a reality that eludes all logic, leaving me teetering on the edge of sanity. An imperfect being, a combination of two different realms but belonging to neither, is tormenting. I can feel the demons watching me, ready to pounce at any time for the one moment I give in and accept a hint of darkness. Like any sin, it will initially feel pleasurable, and I'll start to desire more. Once my soul is blackened by sin, I cannot return to heaven unless I am cleansed. But to become clean means to erase my false humanity. Noah's spirit is within me and gives me my existence. To separate beings coexisting together, Noah is basically a supreme mortal, while I am nothing but a charlatan. Noah never had faith in anyone—not his family, associates, educators, or God. He lived his short life questioning God, and now I question God; the irony. Maybe God resented Noah for not believing in His existence, but why would a being that is neither good nor bad ever worry about such an insignificant thing? The Lord I so blindly serve, I am nothing but a fraction of His almighty power. One's understanding of such greatness is now pondering His reasoning. What will I do now? I like who I am, and I want to gain more knowledge. Although it's a curse, I have slowly grown to appreciate the human way of acting, thinking, and feeling. I want to stay by Talia's side until the very end, although I have slight animosity toward her new companions; if Talia is content, I can accept the new people in her life.

Talia's friends left and waved their goodbyes as the door closed. "So, you like a boy?" I asked with great curiosity. Talia closed the door and jumped at the sudden question. Her face turned red, and she quickly looked away from me. "Do you love him?" I asked. Talia started running to her room. "Why do you care?" she yelled. I was confused by Talia's mixed emotions; I thought humans desired love and intimacy to thrive. I wanted to learn more about humans, and I wanted to feel love; maybe then my emptiness would go away, or perhaps it would make it worse. But I will only find out if I can fully comprehend how it works. Talia's current emotional state must be related to my question about this human boy, "Oliver." I phased into the walls and up the stairs into Talia's room, flew over to her bed, and sat beside her while she buried her face deep into the pillow. Talia sighed loudly and said, "Leave me alone, Noah!" "I apologize for upsetting you; I wanted to understand love and its purpose." "Purpose?" Talia slowly raised her face from the pillow. "Does it feel good to be in love? Does it give you a sense of connection to someone special?" I asked. "Oliver...he's...just a friend; I don't love him." Talia's demeanor was confusing. She claimed not to have taken a liking to this boy named Oliver, yet her face glowed red. "Why does your face turn colors when talking about this boy and no one else?" Talia was one of the most fascinating humans who spoke with such wisdom and grace. However, talking about this "Oliver" made her stumble over her words, and her actions became uncoordinated. He looked like any other human: dark black hair, medium height and weight, colored eyes, and a neutral disposition. Oliver's spirit guide wasn't unique in either shape or appearance. The color of his soul is different from Talia's; he is green, while Talia's is white. No simple being will ever be good enough for my darling Talia. Then maybe this behavior isn't love. It might be the opposite: fear or distress. Could this "Oliver" be hurting Talia? I am always close by, but I try not to be in Talia's sight to give her privacy. My feelings started to show on my face with visual expressions of dismay and discomfort. "Noah, you don't need to worry about me... Listen, I do like Oliver... He's very kind and handsome. I don't know if I love him because I've never been in love before. Usually, I am so busy with my studies that I never make time to talk to boys, and boys never approach me anyway. So, I figured I wasn't attractive, but then Oliver sat next to me in church one day. He asked me my name..."

"I hope you weren't saving this seat for someone else," Oliver said with a smile.

"Oh, no, you're fine," I said, glancing down to continue reading my Bible.

"I heard you started hosting a Bible study group; that's pretty cool, especially because you just joined the church. Are boys invited?" he asked with a smile.

"Hmm, I would have to ask the other ladies in the group; I'll get back to you," I said, still reading.

The sermon started. The preacher stood, signaled for everyone to rise, and began singing.

Shocked by Oliver's beautiful singing, Talia couldn't help but look up at him and admire his appearance. She didn't realize how tall this young man was sitting beside her. He had long black hair pulled back into a low braided bun, dark brown eyes, very tanned skin, and a beautiful smile. But the part of him that shone the most was his soul, which radiated with different colors as he sang. She could see his faith and feel his passion. Who was this man?

A signal was given to "stop singing" and "sit back down."

"Your singing is amazing!" I said in awe.

"Thanks! You know what's really amazing?" he asked.

"No, what?" I pondered.

"You finally looked at me!" he said with a grin.

Talia's face flushed red, and she quickly looked back down. Oliver asked Talia if she was feeling ill because she had suddenly changed colors. She was adamant that she was fine and tried to focus on the rest of the sermon. Perplexed, Oliver left Talia alone and started listening to the sermon as well. After the service, Talia quickly got up to go, and Oliver reached out, but he wasn't fast enough.

"Bye, Talia, it was nice talking to you," Oliver shouted as he waved.

Talia was too embarrassed to say anything back; the two were currently very casual with each other. Oliver always runs up to Talia to talk before church starts, and whenever he sees her, he always smiles and waves.

"So that's how we became friends," Talia said. I found their interaction captivating. I must learn more about this "Oliver," how my Talia has become infatuated with this young man, and how he does not feel the same way. My new quest is to observe and gain efficient knowledge of the benefits of human relationships. Something that seems so simple, an interaction between two people from the opposite sex, a necessary occurrence needed for procreation, yet rather complex because it required steps to achieve the end goal, counterproductive, if I might say.

CHAPTER 9

*D*o people take time to admire their surroundings? I find Earth's subtleties quite mesmeric. It is not uncommon for the sky to change colors. Various arrays of blue, pink, and purple, combined with the visuals of the floating pillows called "clouds," can be considered a harmonious balance. Weather changes every so often, and for a while, white crystals will fall from the sky, blanketing the environment with "snow." Another fascinating season is spring, when it rains constantly, but this nourishes the flowers to assist in their development and bloom; there are so many beautiful flowers. Every color you can imagine, it would be wonderful to be surrounded by a garden of thriving flowers. I can imagine myself running through a field of flowers, an endless field that stretches on for miles. Just imagine running through a field of never-ending lovely flowers with a bright sky filled with the same colors as the flowers around you. Almost as if the sky was a mirror reflecting the beauty that the human eye can't see. I found myself sleeping a lot more often, and I preferred to sleep outside in shady areas like under trees; Earth has an abundance of trees in various shapes and sizes with different designs of leaves that change color with the seasons. Whenever I felt troubled or lonesome, I would find myself taking refuge near a tree where I felt a sense of connection and comfort; I lay up against the tree's base. I might sound like a delusional, strange statement coming from the spirit, but it felt as though I could feel the tree breathing, as if it could sense my distress and try its best to alleviate my suffering. I could not sense a soul within this organic matter, yet it flowed with a strange, immense spiritual energy. Every tree emitted spiritual energy, but it all felt the same. It's as if they were all connected. No, they are all connected as one being, and its energy flows through the world, supercharging everything. Every living thing works together, knowingly or unknowingly, ensuring the Earth's current state stays balanced. An ecosystem that has lasted for millions of years continues to adapt to any change and supports the living organisms that call this place home. Is Earth now my home? Is that why it is trying to help me? Is it conscious in a way I'm unaware of? This world, a fascinating place, continues to push the boundaries of my understanding. If only my dreams could be filled with this much tranquility; although vivid and mesmerizing at first, further into my dream, they become cloudy and filled with darkness and isolation. My need for slumber continues to grow, and I find myself sleeping more often and for more extended periods of time to function properly throughout the day. While Talia attended classes, I decided to nap in the park near her school; I lay down next to a tree and began to nuzzle into its branches. I gathered some grass and fallen leaves to make a natural pillow; it was so lulling. Although it was a sunny day with few clouds, the tree shielded me from most of the sunlight, only letting a few sprinkles of light through the moving leaves as the wind blew back and forth. The sound of birds and cicadas was soothing; I noticed a rabbit foraging around and a few ants marching over a tree stump, carrying food to feed their colony. A strong wave of exhaustion started overpowering me, and I could no longer keep my eyelids open. The urge to sleep had a calming and alluring feel, and I started to enjoy sleeping, but the dreams were becoming unsettling. It was as if my body was battling my mind with this over-whelming need for sleep but a deep-seated fear of returning to darkness. This feeling of cloudiness continues to demand my attention, making me face the same tenebrosity over and over again.

Opening my eyes in my dream state, I could instantly tell this dream was different from the rest because there was nothing but whiteness surrounding me, and standing before me was a giant door. As I walked closer, I noticed a little boy shaded by darkness with a huge grin and no other defining features. We both looked at each other, and I decided to speak.

"What kind of dream is this? Usually, I cannot interact with my dreams."

It didn't answer.

"Who are you?"

It didn't answer; it just tilted its head and chuckled.

"I don't understand the humor in my questions." Honestly, I didn't understand humor very well, regardless of what I said was amusing, anyway.

It started laughing uncontrollably. "You fool!" it said.

My patience was wearing thin, and I started expressing emotions I didn't know how to interpret. But something about this dream was odd. It was filled with nothing but light, yet it felt like the darkest of them all. I had this unnerving feeling of looking beside me, and standing there was Noah, the real Noah. In shock, I looked at myself, and I was nothing but an outline. I did not notice that he was right beside me; was he there all along?

"You confused spirit... I separated you two," it said.

"Why?" I asked.

"Because you couldn't understand me with a human energy attached to you. Haven't you noticed you could speak to other spirits lately?" It spoke.

Now that he mentioned it, it has been complicated to understand the other spirits around me, but most spirits avoid coming near me anyway, fearing they will also be consumed by sin.

"Can Noah understand us?" I asked.

"How can Noah be alive if you have taken the shape of his soul? As a spirit, you should know this, but demons are consuming you. Although you have bonded well with your human and protected her, no one is protecting you. You have been sleeping because demons are slowly devouring your spiritual energy. Humans would call this kind of dream lucid dreaming, but you are not human, and those dreams are a mixture of your incomplete form meshing with Noah's old memories. I was sent to warn you; I was aggravated, but honestly, you amuse me." It spoke.

"Who sent you? God?" I asked.

The shady figure's menacing grin grew even more prominent. "Oh no, spirit, God did not send me, as He has forsaken you; the demon Lord himself sent me. The universe will never give peace in a place where you were never meant to exist," he said as he started laughing uncontrollably again.

In my spirit state, I couldn't express the emotions I was feeling. I looked over at Noah in horror at the expression on his face—a mixture of emotions that I must have been feeling. Noah just stood there with tears streaming down his face, a look of utter shock and an uncomfortable smile.

"Your selfish actions will cause you to suffer for eternity! You damned fool! Soon, you'll be walking right through this door behind you into Hell!" it yelled, vilely expressing amusement.

Awakening from this dream made every nightmare seem like a blissful daydream, for I had awoken in a cold sweat, trying to clutch onto my reality. My time is coming sooner than I thought, and my selfish actions will cause tremendous vexation and anguish. As I curled myself into a ball of despair, rocking back and forth, I began to contemplate my past decisions. How will I tell Talia? Should I tell her? No, I can't; my presence gives her family much hope. I am protecting Talia, and that is the reason for my existence. I cannot let her worry with uncertainty and fill her head with the perplexities of otherworldly matters. I must fix my mistakes and repair my bond with God; I can't let the demons consume my very being, for if they keep feasting upon my energy, I will become a demon forever, trapping Noah's soul in purgatory and will no longer be able to protect Talia from succumbing to corruption, which will slowly lead to her unfortunate demise.

CHAPTER 10

Since I was a child, I have possessed a unique skill—one that was no secret in my family, where many had inherited the ability to see auras and demons. My family has honed their abilities for generations and used them to help with exorcisms and purification rituals. According to historical documentation left behind by my ancestors, we are God's chosen ones. One of God's angels visited their home one snowy night to test my family's compassion, and a stranger knocked on the door asking for help. My family hesitated but let the stranger in and showered them with kindness. The stranger said, "Why would you let in a stranger? Were you not scared that I could be a criminal?" One of my ancestors replied, "I could feel your warmth and kindness from a mile away, and you are always welcome." My family had trusted their judgment, and the angel, amazed, told God and gave them His divine blessing. My ancestors' tales inspired me to learn the art of purification, and I felt a deep desire to commit myself fully to God as one of His knights in shining armor. I believed that no soul should suffer, and I would gladly guide them on their path to face the grand judgment. I remember watching my grandfather perform an exorcism, mesmerized by his grace and power. Clad in our family's traditional uniform—a white, double-breasted trench coat beneath a long white cape and a necklace bearing a sacred lingam stone—he embodied the strength and purity I sought to emulate. He passed that very necklace down to me, and I wear it every day with pride and pray one day to live up to his legacy. This connection to my heritage is something I hold close, even though only a few church members know about my family's abilities. Most of my relatives attend a different church. However, my parents prefer this one for its warm and welcoming energy.

Overall, I found the church accepting and loved seeing new members join and embrace the word of God. This new girl walked in one day, and her spiritual energy caught my attention. I had never seen a white aura before; it was only mentioned in my exorcism studies. White auras are said to represent omnipotence and innocence. I couldn't help but stare at such a wonderful sight before I could tell my parents. They had both jumped up to greet her, and I guess they were just as awestruck as I was about such a rare sight. I was too shy to introduce myself and just watched from afar. One day, I noticed something was following her, and I couldn't see it clearly. I asked my parents if they saw the entity following the young girl. They both said yes and looked concerned. That night, we had a family discussion about what to do about the energy following Talia because we all knew that we could only see an individual aura and demonic energy as a family. Something that has a devilish influence is following Talia, which could put her in grave danger. The demonic energy is weak, but it can grow over time, becoming too powerful and corrupting Talia's soul. But who was this strange girl, having such a pure soul but being followed by a demonic spirit? Why did she start attending church? I need to get close to her and gather enough information to determine if her soul is worth saving. As a family, we decided I would get closer to Talia, try to become her friend, and continue monitoring the demon. But trying to become Talia's friend has proven challenging, as she is strong-willed and a woman of few words. I finally mustered the courage to sit next to her, but she was so repulsed by my presence that she became ill and fled. I walked over to my parents with my head lowered in shame, for I had assumed I had failed the mission. I noticed both my parents were chuckling at my failed attempt to make a new companion. My father said, "Good job, son; take it slow now." Both my parents smiled at me; the look of two proud parents usually made me feel warm and fuzzy, but this felt slightly awkward, like they knew something that I didn't, which irritated me.

I asked my parents if I could attend regular school to get closer to Talia. They agreed, and I was enrolled in school the following week. Walking through the giant hallways bursting with bright, youthful energy was overwhelming. Looking around, confused, a young lady approached me.

"Hey, need some help? My name's March. What's yours?"

"Oh, um, I'm Oliver. And yes, I could really use your help. I can't seem to find my classroom."

"Sure thing! Let me take a look at your schedule... Hmmm, okay, you're in room 111—that's Mr. Stains's class," said March.

She starts walking with me toward the classroom.

"You're cute. I haven't seen you around before. Where are you from?" said March.

"I'm from around here. I was homeschooled, but I wanted to try regular school," said Oliver.

"Homeschooled? That's interesting... Well, here's your room. See you later, Oliver," said March.

She waves and smiles as she leaves.

I waved goodbye to March and walked into my classroom. As I walked in, the professor said, "Welcome, welcome. I am glad you were able to find the classroom!" "Good morning, sir; sorry for my lateness," I said. Looking around, I noticed that Talia was in this class. I was surprised, but I figured my parents had something to do with it. I could picture them laughing at my desperate attempt to befriend Talia and her running away in disgust. Talia looked stunned, which was understandable. I smiled and waved at her. "Oh, you know Ms. Talia?" asked the teacher. All the girls looked at Talia with shock and jealousy, as if she was keeping a secret to hidden treasure. Talia's face turned slightly red with embarrassment, and she put her head down and pretended to read her textbook. "Yes, we go to the same church," I answered. "Okay, that's good that you have at least one familiar face; go ahead and sit in that empty chair in the corner," said Mr. Stain. I went to sit in my newly assigned seat, and our lesson began. I noticed that Talia's demonic entity was near her, but I was sure it wasn't far away.

The class was over, and we were released to attend our next class. I decided to walk with Talia to our next class for a quick conversation. She didn't look pleased about my casual appearance.

Oliver: "Hey, Talia, it's been a while. It's nice to see you."

(shyly looking away, blushing): "Aren't you homeschooled? What are you doing here?"

"Oh, yeah. I wanted to experience regular school for once. Being homeschooled is getting boring," said Oliver.

"I guess that would make sense... if you weren't 17. You're basically about to graduate," said Talia.

"I'm actually 16, and that's not exactly how homeschooling works. I've technically already graduated, but I brush up on things now and then. According to my testing scores, this is what grade level I would qualify for, so I think my parents did a good job," Oliver said while chuckling.

Talia seems a bit confused by Oliver's explanation, but she's secretly happy to see him. They walk into the next class together, and everyone stares at them as they enter the room. They both sit down and continue their conversation.

Talia: "Don't bother me during school hours. People will stare at us."

Oliver: "Why? I don't care about people staring."

Talia (blushing): "Damnit, Oliver!"

Classmates begin to whisper.

Friend: "Hey, March, did you walk that new guy to class this morning?"

March: "Yeah, I did. Why?"

Friend: "I didn't know he and Talia would hit it off so quickly."

March: "Oh, Talia's his type? I mean, she's pretty but weird."

Friend: "It's always the hot guys who are into the freaks. I'm jealous. How do they even know each other?"

March: "Apparently, they go to the same church."

Friend: "What? Talia goes to church? She seems more like the type to worship Satan. Remember those weird pictures she used to draw?"

The teacher walks in, and the class begins to settle down.

Teacher: "Alright, everyone settle down; class will begin."

The students were released for lunch. They had to walk down a long hallway with windows on both sides to get to the cafeteria. They could see the city on one side, while on the other, they faced the park. Oliver noticed a dark energy forming in the park as he walked down the hall. He wondered if that was the demonic being trying to take over Talia's soul. Lunchtime was the perfect opportunity to cleanse this demonic energy. Oliver ran to get his Bible, which had a hanging cross around it, along with the holy water given to him by his father. At the same time, Talia had a strange feeling that something was wrong with Noah and began to look for him; she couldn't explain the feeling. But she felt as though his connection to her was weakening, making her uneasy. Talia knew that Noah enjoyed being in the park and decided to go check on him; she yelled out, "Noah! Where are you?" Several times, she heard his voice. Talia is calling me, but in my fragile state, could I possibly be putting her life in danger? I curled up in a ball and began to weep as I was stuck in a state of conflict, for I did not want to be alone, but I did not want to harm Talia.

Talia: "There you are, Noah."

Noah: "Stay back, Talia. Please."

Talia: "What's going on? I knew something was wrong. Tell me!"

(Oliver suddenly runs up, pushing Talia away from Noah.)

Oliver: "Get away! Now!"

(Talia stumbles to the ground, startled, and glares up at Oliver.)

Talia: "What the hell, Oliver? Why do you keep following me?"

Oliver: "Because you're in danger! There's a demon—it's been following you, and I'm here to exorcise it."

Talia: "What demon? What are you talking about? Can you see Noah?"

(They both stop, realizing that something deeper is at play.)

Oliver: "Wait... you can see spirits?"

Talia: "Yes, that's Noah. He's my spirit guide."

(She hesitates, sensing something in Oliver's expression.). I can see yours too."

(Oliver's face tightens, his awe fading. A crease forms on his forehead.)

Oliver: (slowly) "Talia... listen to me."

(He pauses, his voice quieter, but heavy with concern.)

Oliver: "Your guide... something's happening to him. He's-he's changing. It's like he's... turning into a demon."

(Talia stares at him, disbelief washing over her face. She glances at Noah, her voice shaking slightly.)

Talia: "No... that's impossible. Noah? A demon? He's always protected me. He's nothing like that."

(She swallows hard, her gaze flicking back to Oliver.)

Talia: "You're sure?"

(Oliver's expression hardens, his eyes darker now, filled with a seriousness that Talia rarely sees.)

Oliver: "I wouldn't say it if I wasn't sure."

(He exhales, a shadow crossing his face.)

Oliver: "This is... beyond me, Talia. I don't know how to fix this on my own."

(Talia's heart sinks. She looks back at Noah, watching his form flicker in and out, his figure distorted. Why didn't he tell her?)

Talia: (quietly, almost to herself) "Why is this happening to him?"

(Oliver steps closer, his voice steady but filled with urgency.)

Oliver: "We need help -my parents. They've dealt with stuff like this before. Maybe they can save him."

Talia: (softly, still processing) "Your parents?"

(She lifts her head, her voice gaining strength.)

Talia: "Mr. and Mrs. Cannon?"

Oliver: (with a small, strained smile) "Yeah... they're pretty amazing exorcists. My mom's the best, though."

(He glances away, smirking.)

Oliver: "But don't tell my dad I said that."

(Talia can't help but let out a small, strained laugh. Then, her eyes return to Noah, a pit forming in her stomach. She wonders why he never told her he was in pain, why he had to face this alone.)

Oliver: (gently, almost whispering) "Hey, Noah... do you think you can hang on till the end of school?"

(Talia watches, her chest tight, as Oliver's voice carries the unspoken weight of everything that's at stake). My little Talia had grown stronger; her voice did not shake or quiver. Her words were not fueled by hope but by will itself; nothing would stop Talia from trying to save me. Even in my current weakened state, consumed by sin, I am still being treated with faith and compassion. Although I shouldn't be surprised, my pride has clouded my judgment, for I do not believe I deserve help from such a magnificent being. A spirit with no real purpose, no name, no identity, my existence is a constant remembrance of an unnatural phenomenon; God would never accept such a wicked being, so why should my Talia? It's almost as if my dreams were an epiphany, but I chose to be in denial of my long-awaited fate. I wanted to be by Talia's side forever, but I let the darkness consume me, and now I am nothing but a burden. I am nothing but an embarrassment being confronted by a boy referring to me as a demon right in front of Talia. I loath him and wish for his agony for comparing me to such filth! He will rue the day he dear compare me to a demon; my name is Noah….my name is….my name…my…Why can't I remember my name?

Talia (shouting): "Noah! Noah! Why won't you answer me?"

(Noah lies motionless as if trapped in a trance.)

Oliver: "It seems he is internally conflicted with something or someone within himself. Spirits don't usually have names. Did you name him?"

(Talia glances up at Oliver, tears streaming down her face.)

Talia: "No... he said that was always his name. He told me he was connected to a little boy and took it from him."

Oliver: "A corrupted soul attached to a spirit… This is bad."

Oliver knew the grim reality of Noah's fate from his exorcist textbooks: spirits attached to human souls can't find peace because their existence is a contradiction. Sin cannot co-exist with virtue. The spirit would have to let Noah rest, but it seems they are entangled with each other, and neither knows who is who. One has to let go of the other by fully taking over one's soul or separating altogether, allowing Noah to move on to the afterlife. The demons have probably been torturing both of them for a while, and, amazingly, he has lasted this long. Most succumb to their fate in less than a year, yet this spirit managed to hold off depravity for years. I have no idea what kind of people I am dealing with, but my curiosity has peaked, and I desire to learn more about Talia and her spirit guide. Hopefully, I can be of some assistance.

CHAPTER 11

I deserve to spend eternity in darkness, for I am not worthy of sunlight. I want to live as I am, but that comes with consequences that I refuse to accept. I am constantly being pulled in two directions and having to choose a side, but what if I don't want either? Because of my sinful desires, I am trapped not within a different realm but within myself. This state of vulnerability will lead me to my demise as demons will start feasting on my body; there's no one to protect me; I have no one, for even my Lord has forsaken me with every right. I sided with my ego and went against his warnings; I knew my fate, yet I thought I could be different. For a short time, I was special; I endured the pain of isolation and questioned my every action, ensuring that I understood what could happen if I began committing sinful acts. But slowly, I started forgetting who I was or what I was: a boy or a spirit, or am I both? One has a name, and the other is nothing. It is impossible for something to exist and not have an identity of some kind, right? A marker of some sort to explain its purpose; a tree releases oxygen, contributing to cleaner air and a balanced ecosystem, and bees collect and distribute pollen, which benefits the entire environment and human agriculture. Even demons have a purpose: to cause misfortune and disorder. But I am neither a spirit nor a human; therefore, I must question my purpose. I am nameless and lack purpose, and even God has disproved my existence. It's as if I am worse than a demon. My insouciance in doing as I please to benefit myself has led only to inner turmoil and impure thoughts, ultimately resulting in my corruption. The once unstable but harmonious bond between spirit and human has now begun to unravel. The disparity was recognized early within the symbiotic relationship, but warnings were taken lightly due to an unbalanced ego, unwilling to acknowledge the risk of being potentially tainted. For it knew the dangers but proceeded with dissent into the earthly realm to return to familiarity. A soul taken over by sin is corrupted by a spirit once in control but now enshrouded in sin. A being not stable enough to protect others from sin while also sinning will ultimately cause calamity by mixing purity with darkness. Once all-knowing and balanced, the spirit has now become consumed by doubt. The demon that infiltrated its dreams may have sought to deepen the uncertainty within this unstable being, for demons lie. Because why would God—a being of all and nothing, who is neither good nor bad—want a spirit filled with pandemonic thoughts?

While the imperfect being battles inner turmoil, a surge of dark, chaotic energy seeps from its body, spreading outward. This energy causes the death of nearby trees, which droop and crack; flowers turn gray and crumble; and leaves fall in a lifeless shower. Animals scurrying and fluttering nearby fall to the ground, their life force drained by the encroaching shadow. The once-lush and welcoming greenery now lies in ruin, a stark testament to the devastation wrought by the dark energy. Talia and Oliver were horrified, and both had no choice but to act now, or Noah and the spirit would be dragged into purgatory.

An angelic boy who once shone brightly with innocence and curiosity, his body and soul imbued with holiness, now lies on the ground with gray skin, blackened eyes with red pupils, and wings dissolving into ashes as if being burned away. Overcome with emotion, Talia embraced the corrupted spirit, causing her skin to turn gray. A once-pure human now tainted with sin, Oliver tries to pull her away from the spirit, knowing that coming into contact with the dark energy could cause Talia's demise. Talia wasn't worried about the risk to her life because, to her, she could not live another day without Noah by her side, as he had been with her since birth. To her, they were connected and meant to be together for eternity, whether on Earth, in Heaven, or in purgatory. A being Talia thought she understood was now filled with grief, not realizing how much her spirit was suffering all alone. Talia thought they had each other for support through loneliness and despair, but Noah remained in anguish. As the darkness started to consume Talia, she let out a horrifying scream of agony. Her classmates ran to help, but as they approached, they noticed the surrounding plant life withering and animals lying motionless, a creeping sense of dread washing over them. It was only then that their eyes fell on Talia, and they stopped in terror at the sight of her condition. The pain was too much, and she passed out; Oliver dragged her away from Noah and told his classmates to take her back home. By himself, Oliver was going to purify this spirit. Terrified but determined, he was willing to risk his life to save Talia's spirit, seeing her so desperately cling to this corrupted being as if she were embracing a family member. If a young girl could be so fearless, why couldn't he save this spirit without the aid of his parents? Oliver opened his Bible and began to shout commands and recite scriptures, but this was where Oliver's inexperience failed him because no demon had consumed the spirit. The spirit had brought darkness upon itself by doubting God. Confused, Oliver got closer and threw holy water on the spirit, hoping to provide some alleviation. That seemed to do more harm than good, as it burned the spirit, causing it to whimper in pain. Flustered and confused, Oliver started thinking, trying to pull some information from his textbooks that could help him save this spirit. Then he remembered a paper scroll passed down to him from his grandfather that contained information about a pact he could make with God—a forbidden pact called "The Covenant of the Divine Balance." "By reciting a spell, My soul will separate from my body, allowing me to communicate with other spirits. But with this spell come many risks, such as corruption, permanent damage, or even the death of my soul. I will also absorb the emotional burdens and demonic energy of others, requiring clarity of thought and purity of mind to endure. Without this, I risk being consumed by sin and lost forever." But with this spell come many risks, such as becoming corrupted and my soul being permanently damaged or even dead. Although our family is powerful, we are still limited by our earthly bodies. Time was limited, and the gates of the Netherworld were beginning to appear; I started chanting the holy pact:

"In the name of God, Heaven, and Hell,
I bind this pact with the sacred oath—

—As Oliver began the holy chant, a strange, ethereal glow surrounded his body. Ancient and divine words flowed from his lips, resonating with a power he had never felt before. His heartbeat quickened, pounding in sync with the rhythm of the sacred incantation. With each verse, the world around him seemed to blur, and he felt a tug deep in his soul, as if the chant was pulling him beyond his earthly existence—

"By the divine balance, I seek aid."
"And offer my sacrifice to serve you."
"I will sacrifice my soul and become your holy knight."
May the cosmic forces be intertwined.
Let this exchange be without sinful desires.

I will take this risk.
For if my actions are not pure,
"This day will be my last, for Hell is waiting."

A faint light emanated from Noah's body as Oliver chanted the holy words. His once-gray skin slowly regained its natural tone, and his wings, which had been charred stumps, began to sprout new feathers. Yet, even as Noah's body healed, Oliver noticed with growing concern that Noah's eyes still held their blackened irises, swirling with red. The corruption, though retreating, lingered like a shadow, clinging to his soul and waiting to resurface. At the same time, a brilliant white light enveloped Oliver, flooding the area with divine energy. His own body began to transform under the intensity of the ritual. His skin turned pure and without a blemish; intricate scars emerged across his arms and chest. These scars, resembling branching tree roots or ancient vines, glowed with a faint golden hue, pulsing in rhythm with his heartbeat. The transformation was agonizing. Oliver's new, radiant appearance contrasted sharply with the dark, twisted veins of corruption that had seeped into him. As he continued to chant, he felt the weight of his new role, marked by the divine scars that signified both his acceptance and the cost of the ritual. His eyes, now stark white with no trace of their original color, reflected the divine light and the burden of the darkness he had absorbed. Noah's healing and Oliver's transformation were intertwined, each a testament to the complex balance between purity and corruption. While Noah's body showed signs of recovery, his soul remained shadowed, and Oliver's new scars served as a reminder of the darkness that now intertwined with his own divinely granted power.

71

CHAPTER 12

Humans are imprisoned in continuous misery, with the façade of freedom encased in one's mind, finding a reason for living instead of living for a reason. We are said to have free will, but at what cost—our self-destruction? An ego equal to God but lacking the longevity for our time is limited. I never understood why I had to be punished and restricted in buildings. At the same time, birds flew by, along with wasted time—a constrained existence filled with unpredictable events that could significantly change your perception of free will. A moment of happiness could be taken away with a simple rainy day; a natural occurrence can change one's mood. Why does nature have so much control over you? Other animals do not have free will. Some have higher intelligence, but the act of being able to make unpredictable choices is a curse, not a blessing. The simple life of an animal follows a natural routine: eat, sleep, mate, and repeat. As it ages and eventually dies, it returns to nature, nurturing the soil and feeding other animals, thus continuing the cycle and supporting the ecosystem. Although humans do the same, the only difference is that we think we are special and can cheat the cycle, equating our lives to something better than other species, other people, and even the natural world itself, forgetting that, in the end, we are part of the same ecosystem we strive to dominate. Religion gives humans hope and purpose to continue their lives in the belief that it doesn't end, that their souls will reincarnate or go to heaven. The ones who do wrong will go to Hell or be forced to redo their lives again. Different faiths, some with multiple Gods and others with a single God, view God as a person, an animal, or an object. All have the purpose of sharing stories of the divine and recounting past events, perhaps to improve one's life or to prepare for the future. Has no one ever questioned why other species do not praise an other-worldly being every day? Why are humans extraordinary? Our intellect may be impressive, but our other abilities are mediocre at best. My father constantly states that although humans are a part of the circle of life, our essence is ethereal and extraordinary, and we are blessed to experience two heavens: a paradise on earth and heaven. We are given the ability to fail, love, grow, destroy, and evolve. Humans possess a limitless mind but a body that expires with time, a unified consciousness enriched by accumulated knowledge, maintained and preserved through the ages in written manuscripts. A wise, educated man, a professor who teaches others to think with reason, yet sits in church and listens to stories. How could someone who teaches physics and abstract mathematical concepts sit here and listen to nonsense? I finally told him I refused to attend church because it didn't equip me with usable knowledge. My father disagreed. Angry, I argued back, demanding an explanation. He asked me what I thought was taught first: science or religion. I answered with "religion," of course; people had limited knowledge of the things around them, so they would make up mystical beings to explain everything. Then he asked me to explain what science is. I defined science as "the study of how things work in the world around us." It helps us learn about everything from plants and animals to stars and planets by asking questions, trying new ideas, and looking for answers. He said, "That's a wonderful definition," and praised me for my intellect. He gently patted me on the head, tussled my hair with his big, warm hands, and smiled. "I raised such a bright boy; I am so proud of you." Embarrassed and flustered, I grew irritated instead of taking pleasure in the admiration. I felt like a child because I was trying to win a battle to see who had the most remarkable mind, but my father wasn't participating. To him, I was just a kid who was not worth the time or energy to debate with; I was beneath him in size and brainpower. I yelled and demanded to stay home, my eyes glaring at my father with so much hate and disgust. My rage blindsided him, and with no argument, he agreed to let me stay home; he said, "I hope you find the connection one day. You'll find it much sooner than I did; you're much more intelligent than I was at your age." Then he walked into his office and closed the door.

I remember sobbing in resentment as he walked away, blinded by rage. I did not appreciate the gentle and kind nature of my father, a man who sought nothing but to give his children everything. "Freedom to think and speak one's mind is rare in any household, especially without repercussions." He was a man who just wanted us to learn as much as possible, no matter where the information was coming from, with or without evidence; to him, all knowledge was valuable. "I wonder what the expression on his face was after he closed the door. Was he confused, sorrowful, or disappointed with my behavior?" "What did he do behind that door?" What would I have done to such an ungrateful son who despises every fiber of my being and believes he is superior? So naive, yet that's the mind of a child. Honestly, I was envious of my father; that man was truly remarkable. He was the greatest storyteller, traversing the globe and speaking multiple languages. He answered every question I ever asked, no matter how trivial; if he didn't know, he would find an answer because he always said, "Children have the best questions, and I want to know the answer." I pushed this man away and preferred my mother, who always talked to me like an adult, unlike my father. She didn't like the tensions between my father and me, but my father had accepted my temperament. As long as I didn't disrespect my mother or sister, I was free to express myself. All my short life, I hammered my thoughts and feelings into people, and that made me unlikable. But my family always accepted and loved me. So, when they died, I had no one. Every day felt so long, and I found myself missing school because I never got out of bed. I would look at my father's old books and start randomly sobbing, having flashbacks of my family spending time together. I had a deep feeling of "saudade"; the emotions were overwhelming, and I found myself having panic attacks. I was exhausted, and I had lost so much weight because I had no appetite that people were starting to get concerned. But I didn't want to talk because, deep down, I felt guilty and had no right to grieve. I was horrible to my family, and now they're gone. I hated myself; I was a failure; I wished I had died. They were good people, and I was a terrible person, so how do I get to live? I found myself unable to sleep one night and wandered aimlessly through the darkness, and the sound of rushing water caught my attention. Hearing the water triggered memories of my family and me at the beach. The sound was so enticing that I couldn't control the direction I was headed. It was as if the water was calling me, and the melody of the waves was enchanting—a sound of familiarity and freedom.

I don't deserve a family.
I don't deserve eternal happiness.
I don't deserve anything.
I am a failure.

I continuously repeat these words as if I am malfunctioning, unable to stop; it's as if I am broken. It is my choice to be immersed in perpetual darkness. It is my punishment to suffer and meander forever in rumination.

Stuck in a battle between light and dark, the spirit and Noah compete for stability, as the two cannot co-exist. The spirit can see Noah's descent into obscurity, where grief and sorrow envelop him, fighting against the spiritual aid that Oliver provided. The energy granted by Oliver gives the spirit more control, allowing it to communicate with Noah as a distinct, separate being. Noah, shadowy dark energy, and the spirit surrounded by light facing each other can finally exchange the truth buried beneath years of pain, duty, and unspoken emotions—one bound by human flaws, the other by divine purpose, yet both irreversibly intertwined.

As the tension between them thickened, the long-buried truths, shaped by years of shared burdens and silent pain, began to surface, forcing them to finally confront one another.

Spirit: "Why would you cling to me when we should have parted ways upon your death? You were able to see God yourself, but has that not given you faith?"

Noah: "Reincarnation would strip me of my memories. Returning to my family would be unfair. I don't deserve them."

Spirit: "Humans are sinful creatures by nature, and God forgives them, so there is no need to hold on to meaningless thoughts."

Noah: "You'd think that after being connected for so

long, you would better understand the human mind and spirit."

Spirit: "I do, and I appreciate the gained parallax, but now that we are separated, I have no ego or emotions to cloud my judgment."

Noah: "Do you dislike me?"

Spirit: "I feel indifferent toward you, Noah."

Noah: "If spirits follow a human soul from birth, that means we've been together for a long time. That makes you my family, too. I don't want to lose you as well!"

Spirit: "Do you think Talia is family?"

Noah: "Of course. She's part of me, just like you are."

Spirit: "I have no family. I am a spirit beyond such ties. And no, I do not consider Talia family. You and I were sent to protect her, and now she risks being corrupted because of your selfish acts."

Noah: "If that were true, Spirit, we wouldn't have coexisted for so long. With all my sinful thoughts and actions, we should've fallen into despair and succumbed to darkness. Yet, you sit here and say our relationship is meaningless."

Spirit: "..."

"Noah: You saw my memories, and I saw yours. You've felt my pain, and I've felt yours. We had each other, and together, we were balanced. But you're right—I am selfish. I've been selfish this whole time, draining you with my inner turmoil... leaning on you for support." "And now, here we are, standing in front of the gates of Hell." "I know you think logically, as do I, but your words contradict your actions." You were willing to sacrifice yourself to be with me because you pitied me; at first, it angered me, but I found your presence soothing. Nothing felt real for a long time, and everyone's faces were blurry, as if I were walking in a simulation. Life was meaningless, and no matter what I did, I couldn't shake the feeling of dissociation. A deep sense of loneliness consumed me, but there was always this fleeting feeling of hope; I believe that was you trying to help me, but I lacked faith in you like I lacked faith in my father."

Spirit: "You are wrong, Noah; I do not think logically; I think without ego. I am glad I could soothe you in your time of distress. I had forgotten that we were connected in ways no typical spirit or human would understand. Recently, my actions have become contradictory due to my attachment to you. I have gained insight into human emotions. But you are being consumed, Noah; we can't exist together in this state. Humans are supposed to change; your attempt to remain your current self will keep constraining you."

Noah: "I am aware that my lack of faith and failure to grow will be the reason for our downfall..."

Spirit: "I do not blame you; you are merely human."

Noah: "I don't want us to become a demon, but I realize that if I let you consume me, I will lose myself and cease to exist. I will never have the opportunity to be reincarnated."

Spirit: "That is correct."

Noah: "...But without me, Talia will perish. I've been

selfish long enough... Spirit, together... let's become Atman. A name... it will give you stability, help you find meaning in your new life."

Spirit: "Atman, the name of Talia's painting, is interesting. You won't be the only one ceasing to exist. Combining will make a completely new being. We'll become a Seraphiel Cain."

Noah: "That sounds incredible. I wonder if my father would be proud."

Spirit: "That man was often in your dreams, and your relationship seemed loving; I am sure he would be honored. Behind that door, after your disagreement, I sensed a blend of emotions from him - confusion, sorrow, and even amusement. He laughed softly, as if he found your rage both naive and endearing."

Noah: He laughed softly; "I never thought of that as an option."

Spirit: "Are you ready to be together as God's servant for eternity?"

Noah: "I would follow you to the ends of the universe if you asked."

At that moment, the tension between light and dark dissolved. A swirling energy, both shadow and radiant glow, began to merge, wrapping around them like the threads of fate. Noah's darkness, full of human imperfection, and the Spirit's radiant purity. Slowly, the two forces collided, blending into a single pulse of divine energy. As their bodies became one, Noah and the Spirit shed their old selves, embracing their new, unified form: Seraphiel Cain, a being of balanced light and shadow. The skies above purgatory rumbled as the gates closed behind them, sealing their bond forever. Atman's holy presence was so intense that the once-decayed and dying plant life started to flourish again. Oliver stood in awe of the transformation, falling in disbelief. That something so majestic could exist and that he would have the privilege to see it. In quick realization, Oliver comprehended that the two spirits successfully combined, becoming an entirely new being. One powerful enough to protect Talia and stable enough to stay tethered to both realms without becoming corrupted.

Atman stood still, fully realizing its existence as if experiencing the moment of being born. The being now exuded the maturity of a wise man with a body to match. Once a boy, now stood a man with sparkling wings—one translucent like the ocean, the other black like the night sky, with stars shimmering brightly in the darkness. Holy blue eyes, capable of purifying a soul, glowed with an extraordinary, unknowable power. Atman's skin shimmered in gold, and long, feathery gray hair framed its unmatched beauty. This was Seraphiel Cain, a being of light and shadow, and Oliver, now one of the Lord's knights, felt compelled to offer his help. After risking his life for this being, he was eager to continue serving in any way he could.

Oliver: "Good evening, Spirit—"

Atman, cutting him off, said, "My name is Atman."

Oliver: "I apologize. Good evening, Atman."

Atman (studying him): "Hmm... you're Talia's mate. Where is she?"

Oliver (nervous, blushing): "Oh—uh, we're just friends. She's resting at home, healing from the damage she sustained from the corruption, sir."

Atman (grim, eyes narrowing): "Right. I hurt her because of my selfish behavior. I was supposed to protect her." (Pause) "I must see her immediately."

Oliver (startled): "Wait, now?"

Atman (with firm resolve): "Yes. Come with me, Oliver."

Atman grabs Oliver effortlessly, and they soar through the night sky. Atman's wings stretch wide, sparkling under the moonlight as they cut through the air. He is a being with great power, yet graceful and gentle. The breeze was lovely, crisp, and light. As they fly through the night, the moon lights up the sky, and the stars dazzle as if they are putting on a show. The clouds look so soft, although dimmed in color due to the night sky, but they still seem calm and plush. The mood was so peaceful that Oliver fell asleep in Atman's arms. His exhaustion is understandable after everything that happened; becoming a holy knight is a draining process, but in such a rare occurrence, the Lord will be pleased to have another person as part of His mission.

This journey began with a lost, unenlightened soul clinging to the past and being overshadowed by darkness, for he was a child and knew no better. In time, that boy understood and accepted his failures, admitting his lack of self-awareness. This awakening allowed for growth, leading to his transformation into something far more significant than he could have imagined. No longer a lost soul, the boy matured into a being of balance—embracing light and darkness. The child who once faltered had become a protector, wielding a power that held the essence of heaven and earth, capable of restoring what was broken and guiding others who, like him, may have once felt imperfect and unworthy of the Lord's blessing.